THE X

Haunted

Other X-Files books in this series

The Calusari

Eve

Bad Sign

Our Town

Empathy

Fresh Bones

Control

The Host

Hungry Ghosts

Dark Matter

Howlers

Grotesque

Quarantine

Regeneration

Miracle man

THE X FILES™

Haunted

Novelization by Ellen Steiber

Based on the television series *The X-Files* created by Chris Carter

Based on the teleplay written by Glen Morgan and James Wong

HarperCollins*Entertainment*
An Imprint of HarperCollins*Publishers*

HarperCollins*Entertainment*
An Imprint of HarperCollins*Publishers*
77–85 Fulham Palace Road,
Hammersmith, London W6 8JB

www.**fireandwater**.com

This paperback edition 2000
1 3 5 7 9 8 6 4 2

First published in the USA by HarperEntertainment
A division of HarperCollins*Publishers* 2000

ISBN 0 00 648354 2

Set in Goudy

Printed and bound in Great Britain by
Clays Ltd, St Ives plc

Chapter One

The pale blue light of a Philadelphia dusk filtered through the blinds of one of the inner offices of HTG Industrial Technologies. The room was eerily silent, except for the sound of a young woman's stifled sobs.

Lauren Kyte was in her twenties, slender with delicate features and long reddish-brown hair that she wore pulled back in a hair band. And though she had worked at HTG for four years, she had never imagined an assignment as difficult as this one.

She forced herself to stop crying. How was she ever going to pack if all she did was sob? She gazed around the office. Suddenly it seemed important that she remember everything exactly as it was: The wooden desk with an old-fashioned glass inkwell. The statue of the horse. The bookshelf with its bronze bookends and enameled vase. And on the center of the desk, the clear plastic placard declaring: ONE TO-DAY IS WORTH TWO TO-MORROWS. —BEN FRANKLIN. Lauren remembered that when she'd first come to work for Howard Graves, she'd thought the plaque was corny. Now it seemed oddly prescient—as if Howard had known all along that he didn't have much time.

She couldn't pack up the desk quite yet. But she steeled herself and walked behind it to the wall that was filled with framed business awards and photographs. There were pictures of Howard standing next to Presidents Nixon, Reagan, and Bush. In each one, Howard looked the same—an unassuming, dark-haired man with a gentle smile. No one would ever take him for CEO of HTG Industrial Technologies, a man who'd invented some of the most innovative weapon parts in the world. And no one would ever know it from this room—the modest office of a small defense subcontractor, located in a suburban industrial park.

Lauren took a deep breath and began removing the photographs from the wall. She stared for a moment at the one of Howard with President Clinton. What a life her boss had led.

She turned as the office door opened and Jane Morris stepped inside. A motherly, middle-aged woman with a kind smile and a big heart, Jane was the assistant to the head of the payroll department.

"Lauren!" Jane said. "I've been looking for you every—" she stopped speaking as soon as she realized how upset Lauren was.

Lauren liked Jane, but at the moment she just wanted to be alone. She concentrated on wrapping the photograph with newspaper and placing it in the carton of Howard's belongings.

Jane wished she could do something to ease the girl's pain. "Are you all right?" she asked gently. "Can I get you some water or . . ."

Lauren shook her head. "No. . . . I'm fine . . ."

As if to prove it, she began to remove

things from Howard's desk and pack them up.

"Oh, honey," Jane said. "It's been a couple of weeks now and you're still grieving. . . . Do you want to talk?"

"No," Lauren said firmly. "Really, Jane, I'm okay. It's just that . . ." She swallowed and struggled to keep her voice steady. "I haven't known a lot of people who have died. And . . . I've never known anybody who killed himself."

Jane nodded sympathetically. "Maybe once everything gets packed away, it'll get easier," she said. "There won't be the constant reminders."

Lauren nodded, even though she doubted it.

Jane smiled and handed her an envelope. "Here's your paycheck. C'mon." She leaned forward, touching her forehead to Lauren's, and said gently, "Go home."

"Okay," Lauren agreed. She forced a smile, so Jane wouldn't worry.

Jane headed out the door, leaving Lauren to finish her packing.

Jane's right, Lauren told herself. It was time

to go. She couldn't do much more today. Maybe tomorrow she wouldn't be such a wreck.

She started for the door. But as her hand touched the knob, she felt something in the room change. There seemed to be a disturbance in the air, a presence that hadn't been there a second ago.

She heard a noise behind her. She turned, puzzled. Everything was exactly as she'd left it.

Everything except the placard that read, ONE TO-DAY IS WORTH TWO TO-MORROWS.

It had moved. Two inches from where she'd seen it. Now it rested at a diagonal angle on the very edge of the desk.

Lauren blinked.

The room was silent and still. She was the only one there. It couldn't be, and yet . . . the placard had moved. She walked over to the desk to be sure. And then she got the oddest feeling.

It had moved because Howard wanted her to have it.

She picked it up and held it close. How

many times had she looked at it while sitting in this office, working with Howard? It was a precious reminder of those good times.

Lauren left the office, holding the placard tight. It was the one memento of Howard Graves that she would keep.

That night, on her way home from work, Lauren stopped at an ATM machine to deposit her paycheck. It was a machine she didn't normally use because the neighborhood wasn't very safe. But the location was convenient, and tonight she was too tired to go out of her way.

She got out of the car, walked to the machine, and inserted her bank card. Seconds later she punched in her PIN number. The street was quiet, she thought. The electronic beeps of the machine seemed louder than usual.

She withdrew forty dollars and finished writing out her deposit slip. As she raised the envelope to her mouth to seal it, she felt someone grab her from behind.

"Please!" she screamed. "No! I have no money! Pleeeease!"

For what seemed like an endless moment she screamed. Then a second hand clamped down over her mouth, silencing her. She felt herself go rigid with panic as two men yanked her away from the machine and pulled her roughly into the darkness of a nearby alley.

Terror sent adrenalin rushing through her body. Lauren struggled to break loose from her attackers. She kicked and writhed like a wild thing until she got her head free from the second man's grasp.

"No, don't! Let me go! Please!" she yelled, praying someone would hear her. There had to be someone who would help. Someone who would stop this.

The man in front of her raised his arm. A knife blade glinted in his hand.

Then Lauren saw something even more horrific than the weapon . . . something she hadn't thought possible.

"*No!*" Her scream rang through the alley and was swallowed by the night.

Two hours later the alley was dark and silent. Steam from the grates haunted the street. A neon sign flickered in the distance. Two teenagers entered the alley, their steps unsteady from too many days with too little food. They were runaways. The old industrial neighborhood, with its desolate factories, was one of the better places to hide.

The boy was introducing the girl to the joys of Dumpster diving. "Dumpsters are great shelter," he explained. "You can sleep all warm and cozy beneath a mound of discarded rags or paper. The only thing is, you can't stay too long in one place if you don't want the cops to find you."

The girl nodded woozily.

"Now this one looks prime," the boy went on, lifting up the heavy metal lid. He waved his hand at the putrid smell, coughing a little.

Tina trailed behind him, only half-listening. She was still getting used to life on the streets.

At this time a week ago, she'd been safe in her pretty suburban bedroom. Now she was in a deserted alley with this boy Mark, whom she'd met only an hour ago. None of it felt real to her.

The stink from the Dumpster made her feel sick. It smelled like something had died. "I think I'll pass," she said.

Mark glanced up to the building behind them. In one of the upper floors he saw a broken window. It was dark inside.

"Hey, I know a good place to crash," he said, motioning her over. "Up the fire escape through that window." He cupped his hands together—"C'mon, I'll give you a boost."

With one hand on his shoulder for balance, Tina stepped up onto his hands. She swayed a little as he lifted her toward the bottom rung of the fire escape ladder. If she stretched, she could just touch it.

"Pull it down," Mark told her, lifting her higher.

She yanked hard at the rung, feeling slightly dizzy. The ladder rattled against the building's cinder-block wall but stayed where it was. "It won't move," she told him.

"Come on, pull!"

To Tina, the whole night was starting to feel like a bad dream. She pulled harder and heard a thunk.

A man had fallen onto the Dumpster beside them.

The fire escape ladder released and crashed to a stop. The two teenagers stared straight into the face of another man. His body was hanging upside down and his legs were hooked through the metal rungs. His arms fell to the ground like a macabre puppet.

He was dead.

They were both dead.

Tina began to scream.

"Run!" Mark shouted. He took off in the direction they had come from, toward the lights, toward the city, toward life.

Tina stood for a moment, reeling. Then she bolted after him, her screams echoing through the alley.

Chapter Two

At 3:25 that morning FBI Special Agents Dana Scully and Fox Mulder hurried through a long corridor in Bethesda Naval Hospital. They were following a man dressed in a well-cut suit, whose black wingtips clicked against the marble floor, beating out a quick rhythm as regular as a metronome. Whatever he wanted to speak to them about was obviously considered urgent.

The man stopped at a door labeled MORGUE, opened it, and gestured for the two agents to enter. They hesitated and looked at each other for a moment. Mulder nodded and they went inside.

Two covered corpses lay on gurneys in the center of the room. Scully knew that she would soon be asked to examine them. Before becoming an FBI agent, Dana Scully had been a medical doctor. Now, as part of her job, she was often called upon to perform autopsies.

The morgue was dark, except for the light over the two bodies. The other people in the room remained in the shadows.

Silently, Mulder appraised them. The young red-haired woman, wearing surgical scrubs and a doctor's white coat, was most likely a pathologist. The other two had the brisk, official air of government agents. The man was the one who'd led them to the morgue. He was a tall, handsome African American with an executive's polish and the weary eyes of someone who'd spent years dealing with the intricacies of federal politics. He had some sort of senior ranking, Mulder guessed. The woman, who wore a beige suit over a pink blouse, kept her expression perfectly neutral. Although she was younger than the man, Mulder sensed that she was in charge.

Mulder thought back to the information he'd been given about them back in Washington. It had been nothing, really—their names,

Mr. Webster and Ms. Saunders, and orders to report to the hospital at once.

"Agent Scully, Agent Mulder," Webster began. "Chief Blevins assures us of your cooperation. We regret any inconvenience at this extreme hour."

"We hope that your expertise in extraordinary phenomena will help us answer some questions," Saunders added.

Silently, Mulder wondered just how much they knew about his expertise. Within the FBI, it was well known that Fox Mulder had made it his personal mission to uncover the truth in cases that involved the supernatural and the paranormal. These were the cases that the FBI labeled X-files. The agency, though, had never been truly comfortable with either the unusual nature of the X-files or Mulder's intense dedication to them. Saunders's overly respectful tone made it clear that she was an outsider. And that made Mulder even more curious about this middle-of-the-night summons.

"You're not FBI, are you?" Mulder asked.

The two stared impassively, silence their only response.

The pathologist stepped forward with a clipboard, which she handed to Mulder. "Have you ever analyzed anything like this before?" she asked.

Mulder put on his reading glasses and scanned the information on the clipboard.

Meanwhile, Scully watched as the pathologist removed the sheets from the corpses. Two males, probably in their late twenties or early thirties. Dark hair, dark eyes, mustaches, and faces contorted in pain—and terror. But there was nothing else unusual that she could see. Nothing that would qualify these deaths as a case for the X-files.

Scully stepped closer to examine one of the bodies. As she leaned down, the corpse's arm spasmed, nearly hitting her. Scully jerked back. The dead man's finger flinched, then stopped.

"Abnormal postmortem muscle reflex," the pathologist explained. "Both corpses are still responding to exposure to high levels of electrostatic charge."

Scully took this in. They had been electrocuted.

"Any signs of external lesions or surface burns?" she asked.

"None," the pathologist reported.

"Time of death?" Mulder asked.

The pathologist eyed the two government agents. Mulder saw Webster shake his head almost imperceptibly, denying the pathologist permission to answer his question.

Fine, Mulder thought. It was clear that he and Scully were on their own.

Scully slipped on a pair of latex gloves and gingerly touched the body. Mulder began to slowly circle the gurneys, making mental notes on what he saw.

"Well, it can't be long since the time of death," Scully theorized. "The bodies are still warm."

"Somatic death occurred . . . sometime over six hours ago," the pathologist said. "But their body temperatures have yet to drop below 98.3 degrees."

That was highly unusual, Scully knew.

Normal body temperature was 98.6 degrees. Bodies usually began to lose their warmth as soon as metabolism stopped.

"Where did you find them?" Mulder asked.

Again, his question was met with silence.

Mulder had about had it with the two government agents' stonewalling. He removed his glasses, as if for emphasis. "Look," he said, "at least tell us the time and mode of transport. That may help us determine why the bodies haven't cooled."

Webster and Saunders said nothing.

"Hey, you guys called us down here," Mulder reminded them. "If you want some answers, you've got to give some."

Reluctantly, Webster said, "They traveled sixty minutes by air."

"Thank you," Mulder replied. He moved to the other body and examined it, his glasses brushing the victim's hand.

The pathologist walked over to the wall where four X rays were clamped against a light box. Two chest, two head, Scully saw. The X rays were unusual, to say the least. Where the normal larynx, esophagus, and hyoid bone would be, the X rays showed only black spaces with what looked to be crushed fragments.

The pathologist gestured toward the light box. "The most troubling aspect of the deaths is the throat area. Larynx, esophagus, hyoid bone beneath the tongue, all have been crushed like . . . chalk. Yet there are no abrasions or evidence of tissue damage on the bodies."

Scully stepped closer to view the X rays.

"It's as if their throats were crushed *from the inside*," the pathologist explained.

Mulder turned to the two agents in charge and gestured toward the bodies. "Who are these guys?" he asked.

Again there was no response. The man stood with his hands in his pockets, the woman with her arms crossed in front of her, an impermeable wall of silence. It occurred to Mulder that he'd get more eloquent replies by interrogating the corpses.

Scully was becoming as exasperated as her partner. "If you've done your examinations, why are you consulting us?"

Saunders answered her question with a question. "During your work on the X-files, have you ever seen anything like this?"

"No," Mulder answered. "Never."

Webster stepped forward. With a forced smile, he took the clipboard from Mulder.

Mulder shook his head in disgust and returned his glasses to their case. Obviously, they were done here.

Webster spoke stiffly. "Well, thank you for your time, Agents Mulder, Scully. If any inquiry of this meeting is made, we request full denial."

Mulder smirked. "I'd say you people already suffer from full denial."

Neither Mulder nor Scully discussed the strange meeting until they were at the other end of the corridor, well away from the morgue. Then Scully turned to her partner.

"You lied," she said quietly.

Mulder gave her an innocent *who, me?* expression.

"You *have* seen it before," Scully insisted. "I can tell. You lied to them."

"I would never lie," Mulder told her. Then he added, "I willfully participated in a campaign of misinformation."

Scully ignored his joke. "Who do you think they were?"

Mulder shrugged. "CIA, NSA . . . some covert organization that Congress will uncover in the next scandal. It's not important who they are, but what they have. And I'm sure they have no idea, because they called us in."

They reached the elevator and Mulder pushed the button. He checked to see if anyone was watching. No one was, so he judged it safe to talk.

"I have X-files," he told his partner. "And each case has an element of what we saw tonight . . . residual electrostatic charge . . . internal mutilation without any corresponding external causality. But none of them has all the elements combined in one case."

Scully looked dubious. "But how can an esophagus be crushed without the neck ever being touched? Or a body be electrocuted without any external signs of burning?"

"Psychokinetic manipulation," Mulder whispered.

"Psychokinesis?" Scully said skeptically, attempting to hold back a smile. Sometimes she had trouble taking Mulder's theories seriously. "Meaning, how Carrie got even at the prom?"

Mulder ignored her reference to the Stephen King horror novel. He was perfectly serious.

"Psychokinesis is not an unreasonable explanation," he told her. "It's entirely possible that an object or person may be physically affected by the mind or the will rather than by a known physical object or energy."

"Where's your proof?" Scully asked.

"The Soviets were running tests on the subject for years," Mulder replied. "The Chinese still are. Unfortunately, their findings are kept secret."

The elevator door opened and the two FBI agents stepped inside.

"Okay, I'm intrigued," Scully admitted. "But how can we investigate? We have nothing to go on."

Mulder put one arm around Scully. With the other he held up his eyeglasses. He opened his mouth and breathed on the lenses so they fogged up.

Scully looked more closely as Mulder held his glasses up to the light.

And then she saw. Each lens bore a pristine fingerprint, lifted from each of the victims.

Chapter Three

Lauren Kyte got off the elevator and hurried down the hall to the offices of HTG Industrial Technologies. She hadn't slept well. All night long she had replayed the attack at the bank machine through her mind. It was like a tape that she couldn't shut off. Everything had happened so fast and she hadn't seen much. Yet she couldn't shake the feeling of the two men grabbing her or the terror of an attacker's hand closing on her throat. Even worse, she could still feel the presence of whatever or whomever it was that had stopped them. And that scared her even more.

She reached the glass doors that led into the office, checked her watch, and grimaced. What she had to do next was going to be difficult. And she was late.

Tentatively, Lauren approached Ms. Winn's desk. Elsie Winn, Mr. Dorlund's secretary, was not Lauren's favorite person. For reasons Lauren had never really understood, Ms. Winn didn't like her. She acted as though Lauren were an irresponsible, careless child who couldn't be trusted.

For once, the superefficient Ms. Winn wasn't at her desk. Lauren started to leave her a note, then stopped when she saw the morning edition of the paper on her desk. Curious, Lauren picked it up. She flipped through the front section, looking for a report of the previous night's incident. After all, someone must have found the bodies and called the police. But there was nothing.

"Just getting in, Lauren?" Ms. Winn asked her archly.

Lauren turned, startled. The executive secretary was glaring at her disapprovingly.

Flustered, Lauren put down the newspaper. "Yes," she admitted.

The secretary gave her a self-satisfied smile. "You know, Mr. Graves used to let you get away with that sort of thing, but Mr. Dorlund is in charge now."

As if I could forget, Lauren thought.

Ms. Winn, who was in her late forties, smoothed back her thinning hair primly. "As I'm sure you know, we'll be assigning you new duties—" she began.

"That's what I have to talk to Mr. Dorlund about," Lauren broke in. "I was wondering if I could have a minute with him?"

Ms. Winn sighed and checked through her appointment book, as though it required great effort. Lauren could see that most of Dorlund's week was clear. Ms. Winn, however, couldn't resist flexing her tiny bit of power. "Tomorrow. At three," the executive secretary said at last.

"Can't I see him today?" Lauren asked. She had to see Dorlund before she lost what little courage she had left. "It's really important."

Ms. Winn looked up irritably, keeping her eyes on Lauren as she reached for her coffee mug.

Lauren watched as Ms. Winn's fingers neared the handle—and the cup pulled away half an inch then tipped, splashing scalding-hot coffee all over the secretary's hand and desk.

Ms. Winn cried out in pain and Lauren's eyes widened in alarm. *It's happening again!* she thought frantically.

Lauren could feel her body starting to tremble. What if Ms. Winn knew? What if she thought it was something more than an accident?

To her relief, the executive secretary seemed upset but not suspicious. Lauren took a deep breath and got a hold of herself. Then she reached for some tissues that were on the desk and began mopping up the spilled coffee.

Ms. Winn was still making little noises of distress when the office door opened.

Robert Dorlund appeared in the doorway and took off his reading glasses. He eyed Lauren, who gazed back at him; then he immediately broke eye contact.

"Everything all right out here?"

"Can I speak with you?" Lauren asked.

He paused and then nodded to Ms. Winn.

Lauren moved past the flustered secretary into Dorlund's office. He closed the door behind them.

Lauren had been in the office before, but it still took her by surprise. Dorlund's office was luxurious by company standards. A rich mahogany desk with high-backed leather chairs dominated the room. The walls were covered with expensive silk brocade, the floor with an antique Oriental carpet.

Lauren rested her hands on the back of a green leather chair, as if she needed support.

"Please," Dorlund said, smiling, indicating that she should have a seat.

Dorlund was in his fifties, a stocky man with graying hair. Like the furnishings in his office, his clothes were expensive. Today he wore a charcoal-gray wool suit and a pale gray broadcloth shirt. His blue silk tie was held in place by a square gold tie tack that matched the ring on his pinkie and the thick gold ID bracelet on his wrist.

Lauren couldn't get over the contrast. Howard Graves had been Dorlund's partner, but he'd never dressed in anything close to the extravagant style that Dorlund did.

"What is it, Lauren?" Dorlund asked, his voice concerned.

Though she'd rehearsed what she was about to say all the way to work, Lauren still felt nervous. She sat down in the chair and put her purse in her lap.

"I'm here to—um—give my two-week notice," she finally told him.

"Ah," he said, nodding as if he'd expected it.

"Lauren," he began. "Jane told me about you crying in Howard's office yesterday, and . . . I want you to know . . . you're not alone. As a matter of fact, we share something special." He came around to the front of the desk so that he was standing right in front of her, then sat down on the edge of the desk.

"Howard and I started this company ten years ago," he continued. "And as long as I knew him, he had no interest in anything besides work, and so some of us became family. I was his brother. And you were like a daughter to him."

Lauren looked down. The truth of Dorlund's words pained her. Howard Graves *had* been like a member of her own family.

Dorlund smiled. It was a smile Lauren had never trusted. "So, of course, I feel very close to you," he went on, "and . . . I–I want to take care of my family."

Lauren shifted nervously. This was not the response she'd expected or wanted. She was starting to feel uncomfortable.

He stood up and moved closer. "Stay," he said. "Lauren, please. The company needs you. Especially now."

What? Lauren thought. None of this was making sense. Why did HTG need her, a secretary, when she didn't have someone to work for anymore?

Suddenly, Dorlund had one hand behind her head and the other cupping her chin. He forced her to look up at him, holding her in a viselike grip.

"Stay," he repeated. It was no longer a request, but an order.

She tried to shake her head and found she couldn't move it.

"I won't let you leave, Lauren," Dorlund promised. He was threatening her. Scaring her. She couldn't figure out how what started as a simple resignation had gotten so completely out of hand. What was going on?

Suddenly, Dorlund ripped his arm away from her. He clutched his wrist, writhing in pain. The gold ID chain that circled his wrist was pulling tightly, cutting into the skin.

Lauren stared at him, uncomprehending. "What's wrong?" she asked.

Dorlund grabbed at the bracelet but it only became tighter. He struggled to loosen it, to pull it off. It was as if he were fighting some invisible force. . . .

Dorlund's arm and fingers were beginning to swell. His flesh was bright red and puffy around the gold chain.

As he moved away from her he finally got his fingers under the bracelet and broke it off. The gold chain flew out of his fingers and settled in the thick carpeting.

Dorlund stared at Lauren, sweating and scared.

Lauren's own heart was pounding. She was convinced now that whatever was going on was no more of an accident than Ms. Winn's overturned coffee mug. Or what had happened to her two attackers the previous night.

She got to her feet, near tears. "I–um–can't–" she stammered. "I have to leave. I can't be here anymore."

Dorlund, rubbing his wrist, didn't even look up. When he spoke all the false warmth and friendliness was gone. His voice was brisk and businesslike.

"You've got two weeks," he said flatly.

Chapter Four

Inside the library in the FBI's Washington, D.C., Headquarters, Mulder punched in a series of keyboard commands, calling up a computer file. Seconds later, an arrest record of one of the two dead men, complete with mug shots and fingerprints, appeared on the screen in front of him.

Scully, carrying a file on the same man, sat down beside him. "Mohammed Amrollahi," she read aloud. "Born July 12, 1961."

"Convictions," Mulder continued. "Illegal possession of firearms. Illegal possession of explosives. Falsification of export licenses . . ."

"He had ties to an exiled extremist group operating in the United States," Scully went on, scanning the information in the file she held. "The Isfahan. They take their name from the city in Iran. Recently, they've been working out of Philadelphia—"

"That's sixty air minutes from Bethesda," Mulder broke in.

Scully looked at her partner, glad he had asked how long it had taken to transport the two corpses to the hospital.

"I'll talk to the Philly PD," she told him.

Late that evening a police cruiser parked on Philadelphia's Broad Street. Mulder and Scully got out of the back of the car and followed the uniformed officer to a narrow alley. He led them past loading docks and garbage bins to a decrepit brick building.

The policeman's flashlight beam hit a rust-covered fire escape.

"This is where we found them," the uniformed officer said.

Mulder began to look around the alley while Scully continued to question the officer.

"Who reported the bodies?"

"Nobody. It was about ten, I was on patrol and I just saw them hanging around."

"No witnesses?"

"The kind of people who come around here after business hours don't 'witness' very much. Know what I'm saying?"

Mulder walked back to Broad Street, trying to envision what had happened the night before. Were the two men in the alley, per-haps meeting a contact, when they died? Or did they run from Broad Street, trying to escape whatever killed them? He looked around, mentally playing through assorted scenarios.

An elderly woman farther up the street was withdrawing money from an ATM. She looked at him nervously, as if she were afraid, probably scared that he was hanging around waiting to rob her.

He waited until she walked away before approaching the machine. As he stood studying it an idea occurred to him. . . .

The next morning found Mulder and Scully in the FBI's Philadelphia office. Mulder sat in front of a VCR and a monitor. Video snapshots flashed on the screen. Each showed a person making a transaction at the ATM on Broad Street, the date and time of which were stamped in the lower corner. The footage Mulder was viewing was shot at 9–22–97, at 9:30 P.M., roughly thirty-six hours earlier.

"A daily visual record is made of everyone who makes a transaction," Mulder noted as Scully joined him.

Scully held a file given to her by the bank that listed the names, addresses, and financial transactions of everyone who had used the ATM on that particular evening. "We'll just have to question everyone on this record who was at the machine before ten that night."

The images continued to pass by like a slide show. One person after another pressing buttons, receiving or depositing money. It was all completely routine. And getting extremely monotonous.

Mulder was beginning to wonder if his hunch was a dead end when a more unusual image flickered past. A young woman stood at the ATM. She took out cash and was just about to make a deposit when she was grabbed by two dark-haired men.

Mulder sat up, suddenly alert. "There," he exclaimed. "Let me back it up."

Using the remote, he rewound the tape frame by frame. The shot of the young woman and her assailants reappeared.

He and Scully studied the picture. The two men were definitely the ones who'd wound up in the Bethesda morgue.

Scully checked the time against the transaction record. "The woman is Lauren Kyte," she stated. "Fifteen hundred Franklin, Bensalem. She withdrew forty dollars." Scully paused, then asked, "Why would the Isfahan try to rob someone of forty bucks at an ATM?"

"Look at that," Mulder remarked. His finger pointed to an odd image in the picture. Behind Lauren and the two men was a hazy, blurred figure. It appeared to have a human outline, but then again, it didn't. It looked more like the blur created when a subject moves too quickly for a still picture.

Scully examined the image closely. "Maybe there was another person involved."

"Maybe . . ." Mulder replied. "Maybe not."

Scully eyed him skeptically. Mulder looked at her confidently. She returned her gaze to the screen.

"The resolution's too poor," she said. "It won't help much to enhance it."

"That leaves us only one person we know we can talk to," Mulder concluded.

Chapter Five

Lauren Kyte wound her way through the stacks of boxes that crowded her living room. She was going to miss this place. She remembered how excited she'd been when she'd first found it. It was exactly what she'd been looking for: an older house with airy, spacious rooms and character. She'd fallen in love with the fireplace edged in green tiles and the panel of stained glass above the living room window. The rent was really more than she could afford, though she'd never regretted paying it. . . . But it was time to move on. She shook her head as she saw her cat sleeping on top of the pile of newspapers on the coffee table. It figured that the cat would be lying on the one thing she needed.

"Come on," she sighed. She put down her

soda, scooped up the lethargic animal, and set it on the floor, then grabbed a few days' worth of newspaper.

She took a big empty carton and set it down beside the fireplace. She'd pack the knick-knacks on the mantle—the hurricane lamp, candlesticks, framed photos. . . . She hesitated as her eyes came to rest on the plaque from Graves's desk: ONE TO-DAY IS WORTH TWO TO-MORROWS.

She reached out but her hand stopped before touching it. She paused and then picked it up. She couldn't seem to stop thinking about Howard Graves. He'd been so kind. She'd never had a boss who'd been so much of a friend. She missed him terribly.

Why had he killed himself? she asked herself for the millionth time. She could think of several reasons—things that had been terribly difficult for him—yet none seemed strong enough to evoke such a reaction. What was it that finally pushed him over the edge? And if she'd known in time, could she have stopped him?

Lauren stared at the clear plastic of the plaque, peering into it as though it held the answers to all of her questions.

A knock on the front door startled her, and she returned the placard to the mantle. She checked the peephole. A man and a woman were at the door. They both wore suits and had a brisk, businesslike air about them.

"Ms. Lauren Kyte, please," said the man with something gentle and open in his face.

She hesitated, then opened the door.

"I'm Agent Fox Mulder," he explained, holding up a picture ID. "This is Agent Dana Scully. We're with the Federal Bureau of Investigation."

Lauren felt a ripple of panic go through her. The FBI! Had they come to question her about the attack?

"Do you mind if we come in?" Mulder asked.

"Well, I was just in the middle of—" Lauren began.

"Thank you," Mulder said, cutting her off as he stepped inside. "We won't be long."

Lauren sighed and closed the door as the two agents entered her house.

Mulder studied the young woman with curiosity. She was definitely the person in the bank video, only now her hair was tied back and she wore black jeans, a red plaid flannel shirt, and sneakers. She was pretty, he realized, and she was frightened.

Scully took out mug shots of two dark-haired men with thick mustaches. The two men whose bodies had ended up in the Bethesda Naval Hospital morgue.

"Have you ever seen either of these men before?" she asked.

"No," Lauren replied a bit too quickly.

"Take your time," Scully said.

As Lauren studied the photos Mulder looked around the house. Obviously, Lauren Kyte was about to leave town. Despite all the boxes, though, he could see that she'd made a nice home for herself. A vase filled with fresh flowers brightened the dining room table. A corner hutch held a set of fine china.

"No, I'm sorry," Lauren told Scully. "I've never seen those men before."

Scully was not about to waste time with lies. "I'm afraid you have," she said flatly. She held out a black-and-white photo that showed Lauren being attacked. "This is a surveillance picture from your ATM," Scully informed her.

As Scully had intended, Lauren clearly was caught off-guard.

"Can you tell us what happened that night?" Mulder asked.

"Um . . . these guys . . ." Lauren began nervously. "I was depositing my paycheck. . . . Th-they grabbed me. . . . I got away. I ran. I just didn't want to file a report."

The two FBI agents exchanged a glance. Neither of them believed she was telling the whole story.

"They were found dead," Mulder said.

While Lauren was clearly upset by the statement, she did not seem surprised. It was as though she expected *something*, just not the death of the two men.

"Have you ever seen this person before?" Scully asked, pointing to the blurred image in the surveillance photo.

Lauren's eyes widened as she studied the picture. "No . . . no, I'm sorry . . . I can't tell you," she stammered, her expression belying her reply.

"Does that mean you know?" Mulder asked.

Lauren looked up at him and swallowed hard. "It–it means I can't tell you who it is," she said.

Mulder waited a few moments to see if Lauren would say anything else. Clearly, she was upset by their line of questioning. When Lauren just stared at them silently, Mulder reached into his pocket and handed her his card.

"When you can tell me," he said more gently, "this is a number where I can be reached at anytime. Okay?"

Lauren nodded and took the card.

Moments later, Mulder and Scully were headed down the driveway toward their car.

Mulder could sense that Scully was not satisfied with the interview, and yet he knew that pressuring Lauren further would do little good; the girl seemed scared enough as it was.

"So what do you think?" Mulder asked his partner.

"A woman her size breaking free and outrunning those two men?" Scully asked doubtfully.

"And then somehow crushing their necks?" Mulder added.

He and Scully reached their car and got inside. Mulder inserted the key into the ignition as Scully fastened her seat belt. He could see Lauren standing behind the blinds of her living-room window watching them. He started the car.

"She knows who the other person in that photo is," Scully said.

Mulder nodded. He'd come to the same conclusion. "She's packing," he noted. "Running away. But from what?"

As he started to reach for the gearshift,

the emergency brake, untouched by him, suddenly released. Mulder's jaw dropped as the gearshift, also untouched, dropped into reverse. The locks on the doors snapped shut, and the car shot backward.

Mulder hit the brake, but the car's accelerator slammed to the floor first and the engine screamed. He and Scully were thrown forward in their seats as the car sped backward, tearing down the street.

"What's happening?" Scully cried. "What the hell is going on?"

"Hang on," Mulder yelled, twisting around to try to steer the car in reverse.

The car couldn't be steered. Mulder fought the wheel, trying to pull it to the right. Scully looked on in disbelief as the wheel spun slack in his hands. The car sped straight back, racing toward an intersection.

"We're going to go through a red light," Scully said, her voice rising in panic. "And there's a car coming in the opposite direction!"

Frantically, Mulder jammed on the brakes

again. No response. He pulled up the emergency brake. Nothing. He tried shifting into a lower gear. The car seemed to have a life of its own.

Scully pulled on the door handle. The lock was stuck as if melted shut.

The approaching car had no time to slow down.

Mulder jerked back as metal smashed into metal, shattering the windshield. The cars locked together and spun in a sickening dance.

For Mulder, everything seemed to happen in slow motion. It was like a nightmare—being caught on an amusement park ride that was careening wildly out of control. Only he didn't know if he and Scully would be alive when this ride ended.

The cars began to slow. Seconds later, they stopped side by side on someone's lawn, diagonally across from Lauren Kyte's house.

Mulder studied his partner. Scully seemed all right, if a bit dazed.

"You okay?"

Scully nodded. "Yeah."

Mulder caught his breath. He looked to the other car. The other driver, a man in a business suit, was hunched over the wheel. Slowly, he shook his head and straightened up. Mulder was relieved as the man opened his door and got out of his car. They were all going to be okay.

"That was quite a ride," Scully remarked.

"Yeah," Mulder agreed. He peered through what once held a windshield. He could see Lauren Kyte. She was standing in her living room, perfectly framed by her picture window. She'd watched the whole thing.

For the briefest second, her eyes met Mulder's. Then she pulled the curtains closed.

Chapter Six

Two hours later, after being released from a local emergency room, Scully took a cab to the Philadelphia FBI's maintenance garage.

She started toward the bustling garage where at least six mechanics in gray coveralls were working. But she stopped as soon as she realized they weren't working on the car she and Mulder had totaled that morning. Their car was sitting outside, next to a chain-link fence.

Mulder was standing beside it, frowning. He'd loosened his tie and rolled up his shirt-sleeves. Now he seemed to be doing his own inspection of the towed vehicle. He reached inside, jiggled something near the steering wheel, then walked to the front of the car and stared at its headlights.

He looked up as he saw Scully coming

toward him, carrying her briefcase. "Hi," he said. "Paramedics check you out?"

"Yeah, I'm fine," she replied. "Although I do have a standing-in-line-at-the-DMV-size headache."

"Mine is more IRS-size," Mulder quipped.

"Anybody check out the car?"

"Yeah, it's brand new. Only had a hundred miles on it."

"Someone must have been tampering with it while we were in Lauren's house," Scully concluded.

Mulder shook his head. "The mechanic says everything's in proper order. Nothing cut. Nothing greased. Nothing rewired. Check out the lights."

"They're on," Scully observed.

"They're not," Mulder disagreed. He knelt in front of the headlights, placing his hand against them. The light was warm beneath his fingertips.

"The switch is on the Off position and the wiring is fine," Mulder explained. "The filaments are heated due to the presence of massive levels of electrostatic charge." He paused. "Just like the bodies in the morgue."

Scully's blue eyes widened in disbelief.

"And isn't it interesting," he went on, "that Lauren Kyte was present at both incidents?"

"Lauren was in our presence the entire time we were at her house," Scully reminded him. "She didn't have a chance to tamper with the car."

Mulder stood up. "What if it's possible," he reasoned, "to somehow raise the body's electrostatic charges to the levels we've been seeing and to then use that energy to affect objects?" He gestured to the still-glowing headlights as an example.

"If a person could generate that much energy, their own body would break down," Scully pointed out. "They–they'd start glowing like these lights."

"Not necessarily," Mulder said as he walked around to the open trunk at the back of the vehicle. "There's evidence of this all through the X-files—furniture moving untouched, objects levitating, unexplained electrical discharges. Frequently people who have psychokinetic power are unaware of their own abilities." Mulder reached in and removed his briefcase and suitcase. Scully thought that this sounded too bizarre.

She took her own bag out of the trunk. "Are you saying that Lauren Kyte crashed our car?" she asked sarcastically.

"Either that," Mulder replied, "or a poltergeist."

Scully couldn't contain her incredulousness. She laughed, then doing her best imitation, let loose with the most famous line from the movie *Poltergeist*, "They're heeeeeeeeeere."

Mulder smiled and nodded. "They may be."

"You can't be serious."

"Scully," Mulder said, "whatever is happening around Lauren Kyte is way off the normal scale. And so we have to consider all possibilities. Now with poltergeists, there are three theories: that the psychokinetic actions are totally caused by a living person. Or that it's some ghost or entity from another realm acting through the human. Or that it's a little of both: an entity that's always there but can't get through unless there are conditions of stress in the human. With whom the ghost may have some connection."

If Mulder wasn't one of the finest analysts in the FBI, Scully might have thought he was completely nuts. But she'd seen him crack cases when no one else had a clue. Still, she wasn't convinced this time. Even if she had agreed with his loony line of reasoning, it was off.

"Don't poltergeists usually involve children or teenagers?" she asked. "Lauren Kyte is not a child."

Mulder shrugged. "Maybe this poltergeist doesn't know the rules."

They walked to the replacement car that the agency had given them and began transferring their bags into the trunk.

Scully had gone as far as she could with her partner's strange theories. "C'mon, Mulder," she argued, "look at the tangible evidence. Two Mid-east extremists were killed trying to assault a woman working for a manufacturer of weapons parts for the defense department."

Mulder nodded.

Scully went on with certainty. "When we questioned her, our vehicle was sabotaged. Now, in both cases, someone else may have committed those acts. Maybe the same someone we saw in the ATM photos. The mystery isn't psychokinetic energy. It's her accomplice. If we—"

Mulder walked back to the totaled car and removed his jacket from where it lay on the hood. The lights on the rental car suddenly went dead, silencing Scully's explanation.

Mulder didn't say anything, but Scully could read his expression clearly: He believed there was something paranormal going on.

Later that day Mulder and Scully sat in the car, staking out a small industrial park. The brass logo on the front of the building read HTG INDUSTRIAL TECHNOLOGIES. They were there on Scully's hunch. She didn't think it would hurt to find out who was going in and out of HTG.

A beat-up brown Toyota sedan drove into the parking lot.

"Mulder," Scully said softly.

The two agents watched as Lauren Kyte

got out and headed toward the building. She was wearing brown pants and a vest over a blue blouse. She looked as though she were going to work.

"'Scuse me," she called out to someone closer to the building. "Sir! Excuse me, sir."

Mulder began snapping photos of Lauren through a telephoto lens. Scully sat on the passenger side, skimming through a thin sheaf of reports from the INS, DMV, TRW, and assorted credit agencies.

"She's clean," Scully concluded. "American citizen. No arrests. Not even a traffic ticket. The only thing is, she's in deep with her credit card company. Fifteen thousand."

"That's not unusual," Mulder quipped. He suddenly raised the camera, curious.

Lauren was standing in front of a custodian who was preparing to spray-paint a new name over one of the reserved parking spaces.

"What do you think you're doing?" she cried out. "Just what are you doing here?"

The custodian, a man dressed in blue coveralls, answered Lauren inaudibly.

Mulder snapped a photo. Scully raised her field glasses.

"No, no," Lauren insisted. She pulled the cardboard stencil of the new name away from the wall. "I'll take care of this, all right? Just go!" she said, shooing him away. "I'll talk to somebody," she promised.

They watched as Lauren continued to chew out the custodian. Finally, the man raised his hands as if to say, "Okay, okay, I give up."

Lauren seemed to relax as he gathered his materials and moved off. She moved a little to the left, revealing the sign he had been about to alter. It read: RESERVED—HOWARD GRAVES.

Lauren paused for a moment, stared at the parking space and then hurried back toward her car.

Inside their car, the two agents exchanged a glance.

Mulder spoke first. "She's a little upset over losing a parking place, wouldn't you say?"

"Yeah," Scully agreed, clearly intrigued.

"So the question is," Mulder went on, "who is Howard Graves?"

Chapter Seven

Later that day, Mulder and Scully went to work in one of the microfilm cubicles in the Philadelphia FBI's library. Scully threaded a roll of film through the projector. This particular roll held the last three months' editions of the *Philadelphia Daily News*. Mulder was at the machine behind her, checking out the previous three months' stories.

Scully scrolled through the microfilm, scanning for any references to HTG. The screen was a blur as information whirred past. Gradually, Scully slowed the machine to a crawl. She stopped on an article that had appeared two weeks earlier, and reached back to nudge Mulder.

A large headline read HOWARD GRAVES SUICIDE CREATES SHOCK. Under it was a picture of

Howard Graves, a middle-aged man with a worried expression.

Fascinated, the two agents read the article. Scully inched the copy to the left, revealing the second column of type.

"Divorced in 1970 . . ." she read aloud, ". . . slit his wrist in a bathtub of warm water. He left no note, nor reasons for his actions."

"She was his secretary," Mulder said, skimming farther down the article. "That's three people dead in the last month, all associated with Lauren Kyte."

That afternoon Mulder and Scully changed their strategy. Instead of continuing their stakeout at HTG, they decided to watch Lauren Kyte. They parked down the street from her house. With her car in the driveway, it was a safe bet that she was inside.

Wordlessly, the two agents settled in for a long wait. Stakeouts were a game of patience and luck, Mulder knew. You could sit for hours and not see anything. Or you could fall asleep for three minutes and lose your lead on a case.

Just before sunset Lauren left her house and got into her brown Toyota. Mulder waited until Lauren had reached the stop sign at the end of the block before he started the car and began to trail her.

"She turned left," Scully told him. "She's going toward the center of town."

Scully was right. They followed Lauren's car into the parking lot of a large supermarket.

Great, Mulder thought. *She's buying groceries. That tells us a lot.*

But Lauren emerged minutes later, holding a large bouquet of fresh flowers. Mulder started the car again as she pulled out into traffic.

The agents followed as Lauren drove her car through the gates of All Faiths Cemetery. "Well, now we know why she bought flowers," Scully observed.

Mulder hung back for a minute before following her. In the west the sky had turned orange with the setting sun. The tombstones were silhouetted in a deep ebony against the sky.

Mulder slowed the car as soon as he saw Lauren's Toyota parked on top of a hill. He parked a short distance away, so that he and Scully could watch their suspect.

Lauren, holding the flowers, stood in front of a small granite tombstone. A short distance away from her, a groundskeeper was raking leaves. Sprinklers were going off, sending a fine mist into the air.

Mulder watched, curious. Lauren's face was pale with sorrow. He had the feeling that she'd come to say good-bye to someone—a last farewell before she left town.

Lauren continued to look at the grave. Then she knelt by the headstone and set the flowers beside it. Finally, she stood up, took a moment to gather herself, then left.

The two agents exchanged looks and got out of the car. They walked over and read the inscription on the headstone.

HOWARD GRAVES
MARCH 4, 1944–AUGUST 17, 1997

Mulder was surprised. He'd somehow assumed that whoever was buried here was one of Lauren's relatives. "You won't find too many people at their boss's grave who aren't dancing on it," he observed.

Scully pointed to the inscription next to Howard Graves's. "Look at this one."

SARAH LYNN GRAVES
SEPTEMBER 8, 1966–AUGUST 3, 1969

Mulder glanced around and saw the groundskeeper, planting flowers at the edge of a fountain.

"Excuse me, sir?" Mulder called.

The groundskeeper approached them. An older man, with a bony face and scraggly whiskers, he wore a wide-brimmed straw hat, along with thick plastic gardening gloves and knee-high green rubber boots.

"Is there an office where I can find some information about these people?"

"Who do you want to know about?" the groundskeeper replied. "I've attended every funeral here for the past thirty years. I'm the last person to see them put to rest," he said, strangely proud.

"Do you know how Sarah Lynn was related to Howard Graves?" Mulder asked.

"His daughter," the man answered. "They were at home one day, and he didn't latch the pool gate. She drowned."

"Was she his only child?" Mulder wanted to know.

"Far as I know," the groundskeeper said. "His wife left him a year later. She's buried in her family's plot on the northeast corner."

"Thank you, sir," Mulder said.

"You're welcome."

The groundskeeper moved on, continuing his work.

"She drowned," Scully said, looking at the grave again. "And she was only three years old."

Mulder nodded. It was all beginning to make sense. "If she'd lived, she'd be Lauren's age."

That night in a darkroom in the FBI's Philadelphia Headquarters, Mulder worked on the roll of film that Scully had taken during their stakeout of Lauren Kyte's house.

He'd already developed the 35 mm film and let it dry. Now he cut the roll of film into strips, laid the strips of negatives onto an 8 × 10 sheet of developing paper, and put a clean piece of glass on top to hold the negatives flat. He exposed the film beneath the enlarger for a few seconds, burning in the images.

Bathed in the red glow of the safelight, he slipped the sheet of photographic paper into the developer and gently rocked the tray.

Normally, Mulder found working in the darkroom soothing, a calm, meditative routine. Tonight, however, he felt anxious, curious to see whether the camera had caught something that he and Scully missed.

Gradually a contact sheet began to appear, the series of photographs materializing like a ghost. . . .

As Mulder worked in the darkroom, Scully sat in the office, typing her notes into a computer:

Further investigation into Lauren Kyte's personal history reveals an estrangement from her family. Phone records confirm no contact with her parents for the last two years. Her actions observed during surveillance indicate a strong relationship between Lauren Kyte and her employer, the late Howard Graves. Was this relationship somehow the motivation for his suicide? How were the attack and the subsequent murders of the Isfahan agents related, if at all? Did Kyte have connection with the unusual mechanical failure of our vehicle? I am certain the answers to these questions lie in finding the identity of Lauren Kyte's accomplice....

In his hotel room that night, Mulder turned on a desk lamp to restudy the contact sheet. He'd gone over it several times at the FBI office, but he was still unsure of what he'd seen. Maybe here, under different light . . .

Starting from scratch, he placed a magnifier on top of the contact sheet. Carefully, he peered at each shot through the lens. Image after image of Lauren's house passed as the magnifier glided over the contact sheet. Then in one photograph where Lauren stood at the living-room window, there seemed to be something.

Mulder squinted, pulled away for a second, then returned to the magnifier and peered through the lens a second time.

There was definitely a form in the window, but the image was too small and hazy to make out. Mulder compared it to the previous image. Nothing in the window there. Or in the previous shot. Mulder looked at the picture again. He wasn't imagining it. It was a night shot. Lauren Kyte stood on the first floor, framed by the living-room window. And someone was standing beside her.

Mulder and Scully met at the Philadelphia

FBI Crime Lab early the next morning.

"How did the film come out?" Scully asked.

"That's what I want to show you," Mulder replied. "Though I'm hoping we can get a little help here."

Mulder requested a technician familiar with computer scanning techniques. Then he waited anxiously as the young man scanned the tiny image from the contact sheet into the computer.

The mysterious photograph had a new texture as it appeared on the monitor. The outside of Lauren's house could be seen clearly. Mulder could even make out the lightbulb inside the street lamp.

"Can you focus on the downstairs window?" Mulder asked.

A computer window appeared and targeted Lauren's window in the photograph. The selected image now filled the entire monitor, blurry while the computer adjusted it. A few seconds later the digital pixels formed a clearer image. Lauren's face was in focus now. Mulder could see the weave of the fabric curtains beside her, the delicate necklace that she wore. But the figure behind her was still in shadows, a blur just like the one in the ATM photograph.

"Enhance it by ten," Scully said.

The computer operator maneuvered the mouse. The pixels readjusted, and the digitized image was magnified. Though the picture was grainy, the contrasts, almost ghostly, clearly revealed a sad but familiar image.

Mulder and Scully could see a man—an older man—behind Lauren, standing to her left.

"It's Howard Graves," Scully said. "He's alive."

Mulder sat back, his brain already cataloging a number of new theories as his eyes locked onto the screen.

"Not necessarily," he replied.

Chapter Eight

It was well past midnight. A chilly autumn wind whipped through the streets of eastern Pennsylvania. Leaves sailed through an open window in Lauren Kyte's house, perhaps bringing with them an unseen force. . . .

Lauren was sound asleep in her bedroom on the second floor, her cat curled at the foot of her bed. It suddenly awoke with a bloodcurdling yowl and shot off the bed.

Lauren sat up, fighting the heavy fog of sleep. Her adrenalin pumping, she looked around—she'd fallen asleep with her light on. Her room appeared as it always did. Everything was in its place.

But something in the house seemed different. She listened intently, her heart racing.

Ever since Howard Graves had died, things had been happening—inexplicable occurrences she couldn't begin to understand. She had a horrible feeling that another strange thing was about to take place.

And then she heard what had awoken the cat minutes earlier. These were not the usual nighttime sounds of street traffic or the brushing of oak branches against the house.

These sounds were different. They were unmistakable.

These were footsteps. A man's strong, heavy footsteps slowly climbing the stairs. One step at a time, each one coming closer to her room.

Lauren tensed as she heard a door down the hall creak open. Silently, she slipped out of bed and crossed the room. Careful not to make a sound, she cracked open her closet door and reached for the wooden baseball bat she kept there.

She listened again.

Someone was definitely in the house.

Although the room was silent, the cat's eyes suddenly flared. It arched its back and hissed, scared.

Lauren's heart was pounding so hard she heard each thump in her ears. Slowly, she moved toward her bedroom door.

By the time she reached the doorway it seemed as if hours had passed. She peered into the darkness of the hall, straining to see. Were these just the usual shadows? Yes, she finally decided. She didn't hear anything else. Maybe she'd just imagined it. There was no one else in the house.

Then she jumped, startled, at a familiar sound. Someone had just turned on the faucets in the bathroom tub.

Should she just get out of the house? The thought of a stranger breaking into her house and running a bath was so perverse, so incredibly creepy . . .

But what if he heard her? And who was it?

Her curiosity prevailed.

The bat trembled in her hand as she inched toward the bathroom door.

Then, from out of nowhere, and then from everywhere, she heard the familiar voice of an older man. At first, it sounded as though it were sobbing. Then it rose in a heartbreaking plea:

"No . . . no . . . please, God. . . . Stop . . . no . . . please. . . . *Don't do this to me!*" The voice seemed to be getting weaker, breaking, then more desperate even as it became more hopeless. "Stop! Please stop! Don't do this to me. Don't do this to me. Pleeease!"

The man began to sob again, hauntingly.

Lauren's throat was dry, aching. "Howard?" she whispered. There was no answer.

Summoning all of her courage, Lauren moved closer to the bathroom. The voice became louder again, shrieking piteously, crazed with terror. "*No! No, please!*"

She gripped the bat harder and pushed open the bathroom door.

The sound of running water stopped.

The faucet dripped like a relentless metronome.

Steam danced hauntingly in the dark-blue light that came through the window.

Slowly, Lauren stepped into the bathroom and turned on the lights.

The shower curtain was drawn across the tub. No one was there. But she knew she hadn't imagined it. And she knew that she'd left the shower curtain open.

The sobbing hadn't gone away. She could still hear it. A voice that tore her in two.

She gripped the baseball bat more tightly and moved toward the tub. She could still hear the faucet dripping behind the shower curtain.

With trepidation, she whipped back the curtain—to find the tub filled with water.

Okay, Lauren told herself, regaining her breath. *This is weird. The tub is filled with water, but I didn't fill it. At least it's nothing horrible or frightening. I can deal with this.*

She leaned forward to reach for the drain lever to empty the tub.

But she never touched it. Because two thin streams of bright red blood suddenly appeared. Growing larger, they formed a thick, scarlet cloud in the water.

Trembling, Lauren jerked away. The drain lever rose with a click, and the bloody water began to whirl. Lauren gasped. Her entire body was shaking. She felt sick to her stomach.

She backed up against a wall and wept as the ghostly blood flowed, eerily swirling down the drain.

"Howard," she sobbed. Suddenly she understood. Howard Graves had not committed suicide. He hadn't wanted to die. From beyond the grave, he had revealed the truth.

"Oh, my God," she cried. "They killed him."

Chapter Nine

Early the next morning, Scully and Mulder paid a visit to the Philadelphia office of the National Bureau of Medical Examiners.

"I think Howard Graves fabricated his own death," Scully said as they started down a stairway to the chief examiner's office.

"Do you know how difficult it is to fake your own death?" Mulder asked. "To date only one man has ever pulled it off—Elvis."

Scully ignored that one. "He and Lauren Kyte are in on something," she insisted. "He was standing beside her in the window. Maybe it's an illegal weapons deal through his company. Something the CIA was interested in. That would explain the Isfahan going after her. And Webster and Saunders summoning us in the middle of the night."

"You may be right," Mulder said agreeably.

Too agreeably, Scully realized. "Wait," she said as they reached a door marked ELLEN BLEDSOE—MEDICAL EXAMINER. "*You* think *I'm* right?" Fox Mulder almost always chose to follow his own instincts—even when they defied science and reason.

"Sure," Mulder said easily. "All you've got to do is prove Graves is still alive."

He knocked on the door of the ME's office.

Five minutes later the two agents stared into the expressionless face of Ellen Bledsoe, Philadelphia County, M.E. Bledsoe was an African-American woman in her mid-forties with the dry, somber manner of an undertaker. She blinked once when Scully said they had good reason to suspect that Graves had faked his death. Then she spoke deliberately, enunciating every word, as if speaking to idiots.

"Howard Graves is very dead," she informed them.

Scully refused to be put off. "May we see the autopsy report?"

Bledsoe flipped the report to Scully. "Knock yourself out."

Scully's eyes skimmed the page. "Cause of death," she read aloud, "arterial hemorrhage . . ."

"Four out of six liters of blood . . . down the tub," Bledsoe explained graphically.

"Well, there seems to be some blood work missing here," Scully said.

"We only do those tests if we suspect homicide," the ME informed her.

Mulder cleared his throat. "I don't suppose you ran any dental confirmations?"

"What for?" Bledsoe asked, her patience at an end. "It was him."

"How did you know?" Scully asked.

Bledsoe's reply was deadpan. "It said so on the toe tag."

"Who made the positive ID on the body?" Mulder wanted to know.

Scully checked the report again. "Lauren Kyte."

The two agents exchanged a glance. That only confirmed Scully's hunch. If Graves and

Lauren Kyte had conspired to fake his death, then naturally Lauren would have been the one to identify the body. Scully wondered just whose body it *was* that Lauren had identified.

"Am I missing something?" Ms. Bledsoe asked.

"And Howard Graves was cremated," Mulder said, responding not to her question but to Scully's unspoken thoughts. "So there's no way to run a dental check or get a DNA sample. There's no way we can know for certain that it really was Howard Graves who died."

Scully checked the report again. "Yes, there is," she said, sounding surprised. "His body's tissues and organs were donated."

One hour later the agents found themselves in the University of Pennsylvania Hospital's Tissue Bank. Scully felt herself relax as they entered the familiar atmosphere of the laboratory. Racks filled with test tubes, microscopes, centrifuges, monitors, and gauges—these were the kind of instruments she trusted. Tests could be run, results could be measured, conclusions could be reliably drawn. Only now did she realize just how uncertain this case was making her.

Next door, inside the safe room, a lab technician wearing thick rubber gloves and a clean suit and helmet pulled a column of storage drawers out from a vat containing frozen gas as Mulder and Scully looked on from a nearby window. The technician removed drawer number 312.

"Howard Graves is in five different people," explained Dr. Phillips, who ran the lab and who had escorted the FBI agents there.

Phillips consulted his clipboard. "They harvested the organs immediately after death. His kidneys were sent to Boston, his liver to Dallas, and his corneas to Portland, Oregon. They've all been transplanted. Because of his age, we could only cryo-preserve the dura matter, the membrane of his spinal column." He closed the clipboard.

"So then you do have something that can still be tested," Mulder said.

Dr. Phillips nodded. "And we have Mr. Graves's hospital records. We'll extract a sample, run a test, and in a couple of hours, confirm the identity of the donor."

Scully watched as the technician inside the clean room removed a tissue sample from the drawer. She was satisfied that they would know soon whether or not Graves had faked his death.

Chapter Ten

At HTG Industrial Technologies, colored streamers arced the walls and balloons hovered near the ceiling. A dot-matrix-printed banner reading *Good Luck, Lauren!* hung over the main office area. A farewell party was winding down. Only a small slice of cake remained and most of the champagne bottles were empty.

Secretaries, foremen, and some young executives gathered around to shake Lauren's hand before returning to their desks.

Lauren, the center of all the attention, stood smiling, trying to pretend that she was enjoying herself. It was almost impossible for her to be here after last night. And yet if she'd missed her own party, it would have looked suspicious. Besides, she genuinely liked Jane and a few of the other assistants. Still, she was glad it was almost over. She couldn't wait to be out of HTG for the last time.

Jane pulled Lauren aside and handed her an envelope.

"I made the payroll department rush so you would have your check before you leave."

Lauren smiled at her friend and hugged her. Jane had always gone out of her way for her.

"I'm going to miss you," Jane said, blinking back tears.

"Hey," Lauren replied gently. She handed her friend a glass of champagne. "It's okay. Really."

"Are you sure we can't change your mind?"

"I . . . I just need a new start," Lauren said. She wished she could tell Jane what was really going on. But she wasn't sure anyone in their right mind would believe her. And if they did—they might be in serious danger.

Jane hugged her again. "Lauren, honey, if there's anything, anything at all, please call me."

"I will," Lauren promised.

She made her way back to her desk and picked up the box of her belongings—her name plate, her plants, and some herbal tea bags—and began to head out.

Something stopped her. She paused and glanced toward Mr. Graves's office. His name plate was still on the door. Unable to stop herself, Lauren slipped into Howard Graves's office one last time.

It was just a room now. There were no traces left of the man who'd worked there. The bookcases and walls were empty, the desktop cleared. Any objects that might stir her memories were gone. In her mind's eye, Lauren pictured Howard at his desk. . . .

The office door suddenly clicked shut behind her. Startled, Lauren spun around to see Robert Dorlund standing there, his back against the door. How had he gotten in without her noticing? Lauren felt herself beginning to panic. Whatever he wanted couldn't be good.

"You were going to leave without saying

good-bye?" Dorlund asked, smiling coldly.

Lauren didn't answer.

"Well . . . uh . . . I came to say good-bye. To wish you luck. And to leave you with this little thought . . ."

He stepped toward her and his manner suddenly became menacing.

"I know Howard told you."

Lauren tensed as he moved closer. He was trying to intimidate her.

"And if it ever gets out, I won't waste my time trying to pin the source." His voice dropped to a whisper. "I'll go straight to you."

"And you'll do to me what you did to Howard?" she shot back.

Dorlund froze.

"I know you had him killed."

Dorlund regained his composure. "How could you say that?" he asked in an injured tone.

"He told me," Lauren replied.

For once Dorlund was caught off guard. Lauren took advantage of his reaction, and started for the door. He grabbed her arm but she wrenched it away and pulled from his grasp.

The adrenaline was surging through her as she moved toward her old desk. Her pulse was racing, her mind spinning. She looked back to see if anyone was watching, then moved to a vacant desk, took a breath, and picked up a phone and dialed.

In the tissue bank office, Mulder and Scully were still awaiting the laboratory's test findings when Mulder's cell phone rang.

The technician handed Scully a series of results as Mulder flipped his phone on. "Hello . . ."

Lauren didn't speak for a moment. She froze as Dorlund came out of Howard Graves's office. He started toward her but stopped as soon as he realized that the office was filled with people. He wouldn't risk exposing his true nature in front of the whole company.

"Mulder," said the voice on the other end of the phone.

Lauren spoke with a quiet urgency. "This is Lauren Kyte," she said. "How soon can you be at my house?"

"Why? What's the matter?" Mulder asked.

"Please hurry," Lauren said. She hung up, grabbed her purse and box of belongings and headed out. She felt Robert Dorlund watching her every move.

Mulder pushed End on his cell phone and slipped it into his pocket while contemplating the call. He was still thinking as Scully approached and handed him a report.

"These tests are conclusive," she affirmed. "The dura matter does belong to Howard Graves. He is, indeed, very dead."

This was, in fact, no surprise to Mulder.

He got up and started for the car.

"Wait a minute," Scully said. "Where are you going?"

"To Lauren Kyte's house," Mulder explained. "I think it's time we found out who her 'accomplice' really is."

Chapter Eleven

Though it was just past five in the afternoon, the sky was already growing dark. The wind was rising, and the air damp and cold. Lauren peered out the window and saw dark, heavy clouds massing. She shivered and adjusted the thermostat, raising the heat in the house. She glanced out the window again. The street was strangely empty, as if the city suddenly had been abandoned. A storm was sweeping in, and there was no sign of the two FBI agents.

Lauren tried to remain calm, but it was hard to be alone in the house. She couldn't stop thinking about what she'd heard—and seen—the night before. She wondered what strange things would happen next. It was all so frightening. The sooner she left, the better. At least the HTG party was over, she told herself. She would never have to see Robert Dorlund again. He frightened her, too, now that she knew what he was capable of.

She glanced around, satisfied with the progress she'd made. The house was packed. All the shelves and cabinets were empty. Old sheets were draped over the furniture. Stacks of neatly labeled boxes filled the room. Everything was ready to go into the van. There was no reason to stay, she realized. She could spend the night in a motel and not feel so spooked.

Lauren went up to her room and came downstairs, carrying two tote bags filled with clothing and toiletries. She went over to her desk, turned on the lamp, picked up two small stacks of books and stuffed them into the open bags. All she had to do was get the cat into its carrier, but she wouldn't attempt that until she was ready to leave.

She paced the house restlessly. What was taking Mulder and his partner so long? The wind rattled the windows, and Lauren peered out at the empty street again. An empty bottle rolled down the pavement like a tumbleweed.

Lightning turned the dark sky ghostly white. Then it all went black again with a crash of thunder. Lauren knew that it wouldn't be long before the clouds opened and the downpour began. She'd waited long enough. *Forget the FBI*, she thought. She couldn't stay alone in the house for another minute.

She grabbed her checkbook and a few more things from her desk, unaware that a car had just pulled to a stop in front of her house. A man and woman got out and started up the drive.

Lauren heard a knock on her door and breathed a sigh of relief. *Finally*, she thought. Mulder and his partner had arrived.

She moved quickly to the door and unlatched the slide bolt. But as she reached for the doorknob, the bolt slid back into the locked position and jammed. She struggled, trying to open it as another knock sounded against the door.

"Just a second," Lauren called.

Deliberately, she opened the lock with her

left hand and held it in place while she turned the knob with her right.

The door opened a crack, revealing a man and woman Lauren didn't recognize. They were dressed in dark leather jackets. Whoever they were, they weren't the FBI.

Lauren barely had a chance to respond when one of the kitchen chairs shot across the room and crashed against the door, slamming it shut.

Lauren darted out of the way, stunned.

And then she realized.

Terror filled her eyes as the man kicked the door open. The chair tumbled to the floor, and Lauren screamed as he and the woman rushed inside.

They were definitely *not* FBI. The woman had glossy black hair, pulled back from her face into a tight braid. The man was tall with short reddish hair—and he was brandishing a knife.

Lauren had no doubt that Dorlund had sent them. Just as he'd sent them to kill Howard.

But this time was different. It felt as if

they'd brought the storm inside with them. The thunder was deafening. Lightning flashed on the walls like a strobe. Only Lauren knew it wasn't the storm. It was something much more frightening. And they were setting it loose.

"Get out of here!" she screamed.

The man moved toward her.

"No!" Lauren yelled as she crouched on the floor, her back against the wall.

Lightbulbs began to explode like tiny bombs, raining glass. First the standing lamps, then the bulbs in the wall sconces. In seconds, glass shards covered the floor. The room went pitch black save for one eerie light emanating faintly from the drafting table.

The man spoke to his partner. "Go run the bath," he told her.

The bath. Lauren saw her own blood clouding a tub full of water, then swirling down the drain.

She huddled against the wall, too terrified to move.

They were going to do to her exactly what they'd done to Howard.

Chapter Twelve

In the flash of lightning that lit the room, the man spotted Lauren cowering against the wall. He started toward her, his knife blade gleaming as the sky flickered yet again.

Lauren stumbled to her feet and began to run.

"No!" she shrieked as he grabbed her arm. "Let me go!"

Gasping for breath, he released her. Not because she'd wrenched away, but because the heavy oak dining room table had flown across the floor and rammed him against the wall. It pinned him there, his face a twisted mask of pain.

Lauren watched, stunned, as the invisible force continued its attack by knocking the knife from the man's hand.

Something was in the room with them—Lauren could feel it. It was what she'd felt that night at the bank machine. And later in Dorlund's office. Whatever it was, it was furious. And unbelievably powerful. Lauren felt her own blood running cold with dread.

The man's partner froze. The room was silent. Then the floorboards began to creak, even though none of them had moved an inch. The woman's face went ashen as she saw something behind Lauren. In the remaining light from the drafting table, a form with some definition had appeared. Nothing tangible, but she could see through it, and the light seemed to refract differently through the shape, causing slight distortions.

The form appeared to be that of a middle-aged man. It shimmered slightly, then passed through the living room, moving toward the petrified assailant.

The woman could taste the metallic bile of her own terror. It was impossible, but she recognized him. They'd left him in the tub, his blood turning the water red. She'd seen the obituary in the paper. And yet here he was in the room with them. Right now.

The woman was no fool. She screamed and raced for the door. Frantically, she struggled to open it. She slid the bolt, and yanked hard on the knob, but the door wouldn't budge. The woman turned and her throat began to constrict, as if being squeezed by a vise. As if she were slowly being tortured to death.

Her eyes grew wide and her mouth opened, but no sound escaped.

Lauren watched as the woman's body arched in agony. It seemed as though something held her by the throat, crushing it.

The lightning struck again, but this time it seemed to strike inside the house, straight into the woman's body. She cried out once before going limp. Then her lifeless body sank to the floor.

Lauren screamed. She couldn't watch any longer.

The man got his breath back. He was still hurting, but his fear gave him energy. He shoved the table away and tried to dive out the window. But he couldn't. It was as though he'd hit an invisible wall.

A brutal blow sounded as an invisible force knocked the man backward onto the floor. He stumbled to his feet, his eyes wide with horror. There was the sound of one loud, hard punch after another. With each blow, the man's head snapped from side to side. Blood ran from the corners of his mouth. Suddenly, his head was thrown back and his body rose into the air, as if being controlled by a powerful force.

"*No!*" Lauren screamed, this time an aching terrified wail. She clung to the wall, her entire body trembling. He was killing for her. Again. And there was nothing she could do to stop it.

Chapter Thirteen

"She just asked if we could come to her house?" Scully queried as she drove toward Lauren Kyte's street.

"That's about the size of it," Mulder replied. "She hung up right after that."

The wind was shrieking and rain was pouring down. Scully drove slowly, careful to avoid falling branches that were being torn off trees by the raging wind. "What do you think she wants?"

"I'm hoping she wants to tell us what's really been going on." Mulder rubbed the back of his neck. "Graves is dead. If there's any kind of conspiracy going on, it isn't between Lauren and Graves. But I do think they both played a role in the deaths of the two Isfahan agents."

"I thought we agreed that Lauren couldn't possibly have gotten away from those men herself," Scully said. "And Graves is dead—"

"Exactly my point," Mulder said. "What do you know about ghosts, Scully?"

"That they rattle their chains and say Boo! on Halloween?" she offered, barely able to contain a smile.

Mulder sighed at his partner's sarcasm. "Some people say that ghosts are the residual energy left behind by a very strong event or character."

"Sort of like a lingering electrical charge?"

"Sort of," Mulder agreed. "It's almost as if that person or event leaves an imprint that's so strong that it doesn't vanish when the person does. It explains why sometimes the spirit of a person will linger after that person meets a violent death."

Scully shot him a skeptical look. "*If* you want to call that an explanation. I'd say you're missing some basic scientific proof but—"

"Just hear me out," Mulder said. "There's another theory which says that ghosts are more like telepathic images. And someone who's sensitive to them can receive them—see either the image of the person or the event as it happened in the past."

"Uh-huh."

"But poltergeists are the only spirits that are known to interfere physically with our world. *Poltergeist* is a combination of two German words that mean *spirit* and *causing a disturbance*."

"You're telling me a ghost was harassing terrorists on Lauren's behalf?"

"I'm saying that Lauren Kyte and Howard Graves had a very close connection. He may have even seen her as a substitute for his own daughter, who died. And for whatever reason, Howard's spirit isn't gone. I think that when Lauren is threatened, Howard Graves's ghost shows up and rides to the rescue."

Scully slowed the car even further as a truck passed, coating their car with a thick wave of water that made it impossible to see through the windshield. "This is like driving through a river," she muttered.

"You don't buy my poltergeist theory?" Mulder asked.

"I don't see what good it can do us," Scully answered honestly. "From what I can tell, the deaths of the two members of the Isfahan are connected to something going on at HTG, and that's what we should be investigating."

"Maybe," Mulder said. "But that's only one part of it. When Lauren called me, she sounded scared. And I'd lay odds that what that means is, Howard Graves is due to appear again."

Mulder was impatient by the time they finally reached Lauren Kyte's house. The storm had made driving all but impossible, and the trip from the university had taken twice as long as it should have. Now, the sight of a dark sedan parked in front of Lauren's house worried him.

"Looks like she has company," Mulder said as Scully pulled in behind it.

Even through the storm and closed windows of the car they could hear screams coming from inside the house.

Mulder bolted out of the car. Scully tangled with her seat belt before dashing after him. Lighting flashed and thunder roared as they ran toward the house.

Mulder raced through the open door to see a young man in a brown leather jacket suspended in mid-air. There was nothing above him or beneath him. He was simply dangling a foot or so beneath the living room ceiling. His eyes bulged and his face was bright red, his tongue sticking out as though an invisible noose held him aloft. He was making horrible choking sounds.

As Mulder stared in disbelief, the man gasped his last breath and fell to the floor, dead.

Suddenly, lightning turned the room bone white.

Scully rushed inside, her gun drawn. Her eyes widened in shock at the scene before her. Two dead bodies lay motionless at her feet and the room looked like it had been torn apart by the storm. Furniture was upended as if tossed about by a giant. Shattered glass from broken windows covered the floor.

And in the corner, Lauren Kyte cowered. Tears streamed down her face. She hugged herself protectively, shushing brokenly like a wounded animal trying to comfort itself.

Chapter Fourteen

A little later Lauren Kyte sat in one of the Philadelphia FBI's brightly lit interrogation rooms. Mulder sat across the table from her, his feet up on a chair. Scully stood behind him, leaning against a window ledge.

The room was the embodiment of the disaster that was stark, efficient government decor, Mulder thought. A bulletin board with administrative notices was the room's only adornment. Mulder had a feeling that the place was making Lauren even more nervous than she'd been when they brought her in more than an hour ago. And she'd been a wreck then. Now the three of them seemed to be locked in stalemate. He and Scully asked questions. And Lauren Kyte sat there with her arms crossed.

Scully gave a frustrated sigh. The interrogation was not going well. Neither she nor Mulder had any idea of how the two people at Lauren's house that night had wound up dead. All Lauren had said was that they broke in. Scully believed that the young woman was genuinely upset, maybe even in shock. She also believed that there was a lot that Lauren was hiding.

She tried again, her voice betraying her own impatience. "You know, you're not under arrest," she pointed out. "You're just here for questioning. Now, the sooner you talk with us, the sooner you get to go home." She sat down beside Mulder, her eyes challenging the stricken girl.

Lauren answered her with silence. She wouldn't meet Scully's eyes but stared fixedly at a point on the other side of the room.

"What happened to those people tonight?" Scully asked. "The ones in your house."

Again, Lauren said nothing.

Scully persisted. "Do you have any idea who they might be? Why did they attack you?"

Lauren crossed her arms over her chest and shifted her gaze to the floor. She was wearing the same jeans and dark blue sweater she'd been wearing when they'd entered her house. She looked tired, Mulder thought. Tired and completely drained.

Mulder picked up a photograph and walked around the table. He knelt by her side.

"Do you know who this is?" he asked gently.

He showed her the photograph—the one of Howard Graves in the window of her house.

Lauren didn't get a chance to answer. The door to the interrogation room opened, and Webster, the man who had gotten Mulder and Scully involved in the case, entered the room with a Philadelphia FBI agent named Thomas.

"Scully, Mulder," Webster gestured, indicating that he wanted to talk to them outside. Neither Scully nor Mulder moved. They didn't trust Webster, and they weren't about to leave him alone with Lauren.

Webster nodded toward Thomas and when he spoke his voice was angry. "Don't worry.

He'll keep an eye on her. Come on. Now!"

Reluctantly, the two FBI agents stood up. Mulder grabbed his jacket and they followed him into the hallway, where they saw Saunders waiting, dressed in a pink business suit.

Who were these two? Mulder wondered. And what gave them the authority to disrupt an FBI interrogation?

Saunders didn't bother to explain. "You've seriously compromised our investigation," she said angrily.

Mulder refused to be intimidated. "We were following leads pertaining to an X-file," he informed them.

"I want to know every detail of your activities concerning this case," Webster demanded.

"What case?" Scully shot back. "You're the ones who've been withholding information. Why don't you tell us what you've got?"

Webster and Saunders stared at them as if they hadn't understood the question.

"Fine. Then we have nothing more to talk about," Mulder concluded.

As he and Scully started back toward the interrogation room, Saunders stepped forward. "Wait," she said. "We believe HTG Industrial Technologies sold restricted weapons parts to the Isfahan."

"Partial serial numbers from their invoice manifests were recovered in the wreckage of the July bombing of a Navy transport van," Webster explained.

"How is Lauren Kyte involved?" Mulder asked.

"We don't quite know," Webster told him. "Your actions impeded our investigation."

Saunders nodded toward the interrogation room. "In any case, we don't have enough evidence to hold her," she admitted. "But if she doesn't talk, she goes free. And we lose our chance to break HTG."

"I can make her talk," Webster asserted, a threat in his voice.

Mulder flashed him a wry smile. "My advice to you is . . . don't get rough with her."

Chapter Fifteen

Mulder and Scully stood outside the interrogation room, waiting while Webster, Saunders, and Thomas questioned Lauren. Mulder knew it wouldn't be long before they gave up. The two CIA agents—if that's what they were—weren't going to get much out of her. He glanced at his watch. By his calculations it was only a matter of minutes before the interview would be over.

The door to the interrogation room opened and the three agents marched out, frustrated and furious.

"Well, that was a complete waste of time," Saunders snapped.

Mulder smiled to himself. It had taken even less time than he had guessed.

Webster gestured angrily for Mulder and

Scully to go back in. "Your turn," he said.

Mulder and Scully went back into the interrogation room. Lauren Kyte sat at the table, her arms stretched out in front of her, hands clasped.

"Lauren," Scully began.

Lauren didn't even look up. "I won't talk to you either," she said.

"Okay," Mulder replied calmly. "Then you're free to go."

Looking surprised, Lauren stood up. She started toward the door, then stopped. She took a shuddering breath and shook her head.

"I can't go back to that house," she said, her voice barely audible.

"Why?" Mulder asked her. "Because of Howard Graves?"

"He's dead," Lauren said.

Mulder nodded. "I know."

Her eyes turned to him, searching his face as if she were looking for someone to trust.

"He's watching over you, isn't he?" Mulder asked.

Lauren didn't answer, but her stricken expression told Mulder that he was right.

To Mulder it was clear that Lauren needed a break. He went out and got some fresh coffee for the three of them before they sat down again. He felt certain that this time she would talk. He knew that she had to tell someone what was going on. She desperately needed someone whom she could trust. He had a feeling that the last person she had truly trusted was Howard Graves.

Mulder offered Lauren a cup of coffee.

"No thanks," she said.

He gestured to the tape recorder on the table. "Is it okay if we turn this on?"

She nodded nervously.

"Okay," he told her. "What if this time we hold off on the questions. Why don't you just tell us what you want to, okay?"

Lauren nodded again. But it was a while before she actually was able to bring herself to speak. When she finally began, she was standing in a corner of the room, leaning against the wall for support.

"I don't know if you've ever been a secretary," she began. "Sometimes your boss can talk as if you weren't even in the room. Like you're not a person. And that can hurt, you know? And then sometimes . . . you're all he has to talk to. Which was how it always was with me and Howard."

She stopped as if lost in memories, then forced herself to go on. "One night, late, I went into his office. He was crying, more scared than sad. And he told me . . . the defense budget was cut back and Pentagon contracts were being canceled. The company was going under. Howard felt personally responsible for each of his employees. Seeing and feeling their fear every day really wore him down.

"There was this one time, Dorlund came to him. With that group . . . the Mideast group—the Isfahan—" Lauren walked over to the bulletin board and nervously began to play with the pushpins. "That terrorist group.

They'd buy parts at an outrageous price. Not just once, but for as long as they could get away with it.

"That night, Howard was crying," she went on. "He'd just found out that the Isfahan had claimed responsibility for killing a couple of sailors in Florida. He thought . . . he was pretty sure they'd used explosives they'd made from HTG parts. He was never the same after that. And I thought that's why he killed himself."

Mulder nodded. "A company going under, with its main hope of salvation being clients who are terrorists."

Lauren's eyes met Mulder's. "I believed that's why he killed himself, but I was wrong. He didn't. . . . I saw . . ." She hesitated, as if realizing the implausibility of what she was about to say. Then she spoke in a clear, determined tone.

"Howard showed me how Dorlund had him killed. Dorlund made it look like a suicide because he could see that Howard was going to put an end to the deal with the Isfahan."

Scully and Mulder exchanged a glance.

"So, now Howard is protecting you?" Mulder asked.

Lauren leaned back against the wall, her eyes closed. "That sounds so ridiculous."

"But you believe it," Scully said.

"He was closer to me than my own father," Lauren explained. "I told him that. I still feel his presence. Sometimes . . . I even smell his aftershave." She swallowed hard, on the verge of breaking down. "If you just could have seen the things I've seen. . . ."

She was fighting back tears. "But I just want all this to go away. That's why I'm leaving. Maybe now he can move on."

Scully got to her feet. "That's not enough," she said in a strong voice. She moved closer to Lauren and said softly, but with conviction, "You have been given the chance to tell him again. *Take it.* Tell him you love him . . . by showing him . . . by helping us finish his unfinished business."

Mulder sat quietly, stunned by Scully's words. They were so unlike Dana Scully, who rarely gave credence to paranormal theories.

"Lauren," Scully asked gently, "how will you ever be able to rest if he never can?"

For a long time Lauren didn't answer; then she finally nodded and said, "Okay." She put her hands over her tear-streaked face.

"I'm a mess," she told them shakily. "I'm going to—um—wash up."

When she left the room Mulder turned to his partner. "What are you doing, Scully? You don't believe—"

"Mulder, there's no such thing as ghosts or psychokinesis," Scully explained. "I'm sure there's a scientific explanation for what Lauren's experienced. But I believe that she believes. And right now my priority is to get her to help us stop Dorlund."

"Well, we may have just sacrificed our best opportunity to observe spectral phenomena—"

"No, I'm giving us the chance to solve a case that's tangible," Scully broke in, putting an end to the argument. "Instead of chasing after shadows."

Chapter Sixteen

They all had the routine down. They'd practiced dozens of times. Yet there was an undeniable tension in the air as the Philadelphia FBI agent slipped on an FBI windbreaker, then watched another agent load his sidearm. The officers were gathered at headquarters, preparing for a sweep. All wore identical blue jackets with the FBI logo in gold lettering.

Mulder and Scully made their way through the team of agents to the garage where Saunders, Webster, and Lauren Kyte were waiting.

Mulder ignored the two government agents and focused on Lauren. She stood beside one of the cars, looking uneasy. She had told Mulder that she'd never wanted to see Dorlund again. Despite his assurances that she would be protected, the meeting obviously worried her.

"Are you ready?"

Lauren answered with a quick nod.

Scully took the lead, addressing the team. "All right, everybody," she announced, holding up the judge's order. "We have a warrant to search the premises of HTG for evidence pertaining to the sale of restricted manufactured weapons parts to terrorist organizations. The evidence may be in the form of falsified export licenses, parts manifests, communiqués. It could be on computer disk or hard copy."

"Once there, if in doubt, ask," Webster added. "We need this operation to be clean. This is the culmination of a year-long investigation."

The agents listened intently as Webster described the stakes involved. "If we don't come out of there today with something proving a connection to the Isfahan, then Dorlund could walk."

"Okay," Scully said, "let's go."

The agents dispersed. Mulder went up to

Lauren, who was becoming more visibly nervous by the second.

"Lauren, are you all right?"

She nodded.

Scully put a hand on Lauren's back, guiding her to their car. "The proof we're looking for will most likely be in Dorlund's office," Scully told her. "We'll execute the search, but we need you to guide us so you have to be strong. Okay?"

Lauren nodded, took a deep breath and got into the car. Mulder thought she had never seemed more fragile.

Less than thirty minutes later, the FBI team entered the offices of HTG Industrial Technologies. The agents swept into the main office, quickly dispersing to assigned areas. Scully, leading the way, issued polite but firm orders to the employees.

"Everybody, stay calm," she called out. "Federal Bureau of Investigation. Ma'am, could you back away from those files, please?"

"Step aside, please," Webster called, clearly in his element.

In a matter of seconds, drawers were pulled open, files were emptied, disks were taken from computers.

Through it all, the employees of HTG stood back, looking startled and surprised.

Dorlund, hearing the commotion in the outer offices, opened his office door. Mulder noted that his face drained of all color, but he didn't say a word as Scully and Lauren marched past him into his office.

Webster followed and went straight to one of Dorlund's file cabinets, where he began searching through the top drawer. It soon became clear that he wasn't finding what he wanted. Coming up empty, he slammed the drawer shut.

One of the FBI agents flipped through papers in a stack of cardboard cartons. Nothing. He checked another box. A second agent sat down at Dorlund's computer, where he called up the file utility and scanned the contents of the hard drive, then typed in the command to reveal hidden files. Mulder watched as the agent inserted an FBI disk that searched for encrypted files. If Dorlund had the evidence here, they would find it. Yet Mulder was starting to have serious doubts that there was anything to find.

What worried him was that Dorlund didn't look concerned. In fact, he looked cool, calm, and confident. Mulder never doubted Dorlund's guilt—he was convinced that Lauren was telling the truth. But it occurred to him that the evidence might not be in the offices. What if Dorlund kept his records in a safe deposit box on the other side of town, or in another country? What if he was smart enough not to leave any kind of paper or electronic trail?

Scully kept searching. With Lauren by her side, she went through the file cabinets and searched the drawers of Dorlund's desk. Lauren, Mulder saw, was getting more frantic by the second. The search mattered more to her than it did to any of them. This was her one chance to stop Dorlund and put Howard Graves's troubled spirit to rest. As it became clear that the search was failing, Lauren became more and more agitated.

Scully opened the door to the low cabinets that lined the wall. They were filled with books. She and Lauren began to riffle through them, to see if anything was hidden in their pages. As they finished with each book, they tossed it to the ground and grabbed another. Though his office was being torn apart, Dorlund stood watching, calm and eerily composed.

Twenty minutes later, Saunders and Webster approached Mulder. They gestured to the FBI agents behind them, who held a few small cartons filled with papers.

"This is all we could find," Saunders said, sounding disgusted.

Mulder glanced at Dorlund, who was reassuring some of his employees. "We don't have him," Mulder said, not even bothering to look at the boxes. Dorlund's demeanor spoke volumes. "He hasn't sweat a drop."

"Our case is blown," Webster said accusingly. "We wasted a year. Dorlund's going to walk."

Chapter Seventeen

Mulder watched as Webster and Saunders and most of the FBI sweep team left. He refused to feel guilty about the government's case being blown. That was hardly his fault or Scully's. But it bothered him that Robert Dorlund was literally getting away with murder—and that Lauren Kyte would spend the rest of her life terrified of what he might do to her. Or of what Howard Graves's ghost might do to protect her.

Frustrated, Mulder headed back into Dorlund's office. It was time to get Lauren away from HTG.

Scully turned to Mulder as he entered. She shook her head and sighed. Nothing. She grabbed a box of paperwork—something that might contain a clue—but Mulder could tell that she wasn't pinning any real hope on it.

"Let's get out of here," she said, looking defeated.

Dorlund entered the office and leaned against a file cabinet.

Lauren, however, wouldn't give up. Trembling with frustration and anger, she removed one of the framed photographs from the wall. With a brass letter opener she ripped the backing apart, throwing the picture to the floor. Then reached for another.

"Lauren, it's over," Mulder said. "We have to go. What we're looking for isn't here."

Lauren didn't even seem to hear him. She smashed through the glass of another framed photograph.

Dorlund spoke for the first time. "Hey!" he objected angrily. "*She's* not an agent! Look, I've been more than cooperative, and I don't want to be combative, but she's got no right to destroy my personal property."

"Lauren—" Mulder warned.

Lauren whirled on Dorlund furiously. "'Destroying property'?" she echoed. "What about that van that blew up and killed those Navy men?"

She obviously hit a nerve. Dorlund dropped all pretense of being polite and in control. "I don't know what the hell you're talking about, you stupid bitch!" he yelled, starting toward her.

Furious, Lauren went for Dorlund, brandishing the letter opener like a knife.

"Lauren, no!" Mulder shouted.

He broke toward Lauren, whose arm was raised to strike. But Dorlund got to her first. He grabbed her by the arm and twisted hard, forcing her to drop the letter opener.

Suddenly, Dorlund released Lauren and jerked backward. His head hit the wall. His hands flew back against it, as if pinned in surrender. The office door slammed shut.

Dorlund's expression changed from rage to terror. His face reddened and his throat contracted, as if someone had their hands around his neck, squeezing with incredible force. Gasping, he reached for his throat, but he couldn't relieve the agony.

Mulder and Lauren watched in stunned disbelief. Lauren recovered first, realizing what was happening.

"Don't kill him!" she pleaded with Howard Graves. "Help us find it, instead!"

Dorlund's pain seemed to ease. He dropped to the floor, gasping for breath.

Mulder wondered what would happen next.

He got his answer soon enough. One after another, the lightbulbs in the office began to explode.

"Get down!" Mulder shouted, pulling Lauren with him to the side of the desk. They crouched for cover as glass rained down all around them. The room was vibrating with power.

Outside Dorlund's office, Scully, hearing the commotion, ran toward the closed door.

"Mulder!" she cried. She tried to pull the door open but it wouldn't budge. It was as though it had been welded shut.

x x x

Inside Dorlund's office, Mulder watched as framed photographs flew off the wall. Desk drawers popped open. Papers spewed out into the air as though a hurricane were whirling inside the room. Hundreds of papers swirled above as objects seemed to momentarily take on a life of their own.

Mulder and Lauren huddled together in the eye of the storm. Frozen in awe, they were stunned as the room was taken over by the vortex of frenetic energy.

The letter opener flew straight toward Robert Dorlund's throat and hovered there less than an inch from his skin, as if deciding whether or not to impale him.

Mulder watched in amazement as the letter opener suddenly changed direction. It turned sharply to the right and flew into the fabric-covered wall—where it gashed a straight line through the silk brocade.

The energy suddenly left the room. The storm stopped as suddenly as it had started, and everything was still.

The door to the office burst open and Scully rushed in. She stopped, frozen by the chaos surrounding her. Dorlund lay on the floor, coughing. Mulder and Lauren were crouched behind the desk. And the office looked a lot like Lauren's house had looked the night before.

"My God," Scully gasped. "What happened?"

"Lauren, are you all right?" Mulder asked.

She nodded, a little dazed, then turned to stare at the tear in the wall. The letter opener stuck there, embedded, motionless.

Mulder stood up slowly. Curious, he walked over to the wall where the fabric had been torn.

He pulled the silk away from the wall and removed a small micro disk that had been taped there. Mulder held up the disk and looked at his partner. "I guess it was here after all," he said.

Chapter Eighteen

That same evening, Scully and Mulder made one last trip to Lauren Kyte's house. They got there just in time. Despite the late hour, Lauren was moving. A padlocked trailer was hitched to the back of her car. When they arrived, she was carrying one last carton out of the house.

"The U.S. Attorney's office is going after Dorlund with everything they've got," Scully assured her. "Including the murder of Howard Graves."

Lauren nodded and set the box in the open trunk of her car. "I'll come back to testify," she told them.

"Where are you going?" Mulder asked.

"Away from here." she answered.

Mulder wondered how serious she was

about testifying when she didn't even bother to tell them where she was moving to. Maybe she didn't know. She'd done what she had needed to in order to put Howard Graves's spirit to rest; now there was no reason to stay. All that mattered was leaving, putting as much distance as she could between herself and her memories.

Lauren shut the trunk and got into the car. She started the engine and shifted into reverse. Then almost as an afterthought, she stuck her head out the window.

"Thanks," she called out to the agents. Then she drove off, leaving Mulder and Scully standing in the darkened street.

"Boy, she's in a rush to get out of here," Mulder observed.

"Out of here?" Scully asked, teasingly. "Or away from the ghost of Howard Graves?"

Mulder looked at his partner curiously.

"Hey, Scully, do you believe in an afterlife?"

"I'd settle for a life in this one," she answered with a smile.

Her response made Mulder think of the

plastic plaque that had been on Lauren's mantle. Something about one today being worth two tomorrows.

"Have you ever seen the Liberty Bell?" he asked.

"Yes," Scully replied, getting into the car.

Mulder got in on the driver's side. "You know," he admitted as he fastened his seat belt, "I've been to Philadelphia a hundred times and I've never seen it."

"Honestly, you're not missing much," Scully told him. "It's a big bell. With a big crack. And you have to wait in a long line to see it."

"Yeah, but . . . I think I'd really like to go."

"Why now?"

"I don't know," he answered. "How late do you think they stay open?"

Mulder smiled to himself. It was something he would rather not explain, but somehow their encounter with the ghost of Howard Graves had reminded him that life was far too brief to waste.

x x x

Lauren Kyte assembled a handful of papers from assorted files and placed them in a blue presentation folder. Two months had passed since she left Philadelphia. She was working for the Monroe Mutual Insurance Company in Omaha, Nebraska. The job wasn't exactly exciting, but then again, that was partly why she'd chosen it. No secretive high-tech defense work. No chance of dealing with terrorists or FBI investigations. Her life was simple—processing insurance claims in a sleepy, Midwest town.

She even felt different now. When she looked in the mirror she saw the same features—but without the tension that had been there in Philadelphia.

At the moment, she was behind on a deadline. She straightened the papers in their folder and hurried over to Ms. Lange, the boss's secretary. That was the only weird thing about this place, Lauren thought. Ms. Lange reminded her of Dorlund's secretary, Ms. Winn. They had the same stickler-for-details manner, the overblown self-importance. Even worse, Ms. Lange seemed to have a bone-deep mistrust of anyone who came from the East.

Ms. Lange frowned as Lauren handed her the folder. "Miss Kyte, I asked for this twenty-five minutes ago," she snapped.

"I know . . . I'm sorry," Lauren mumbled.

Ms. Lange wasn't about to accept her apology. She pursed her lips in disapproval. "Maybe they work that way back East, but here in the Midwest, punctuality is a virtue."

She reached for her coffee cup, and Lauren felt her body tense as something in the air shifted.

At that moment, Ms. Lange's coffee mug began to vibrate harder and harder, until it was nearly bouncing on the desktop.

Lauren couldn't believe it. He was here.

Ms. Lange reached out and steadied the mug. "We have to find new office space," she remarked. "Every time a truck passes on the street, the whole building shakes!"

Lauren felt herself relax as Ms. Lange

sipped her coffee. The air felt different now. He was gone. Or maybe he'd never been here. Maybe it *was* just a truck.

"That's all, Lauren," Ms. Lange said crisply.

Lauren returned to her desk and went back to work. But a few moments later, she paused to gaze on the familiar plastic placard that sat on her desk. She couldn't help wondering about her todays and her tomorrows—and whether the ghost of Howard Graves would still be part of them.

Don't miss the next *X-Files* Young Adult book:

#16 *Miracle Man*

by Terry Bisson

The town of Kenwood, Tennessee, hadn't seen this much excitement in years. Not since Elvis had driven through in his pink Cadillac, thirty years earlier.

Elvis had made it.

This Caddy hadn't.

Speeding, it had swerved to miss another car, bounced off a van, and hit a telephone pole. Then it burst into flames.

Now Kenwood's usually sleepy Main Street was littered with broken glass and twisted steel, and jammed with fire trucks, police cars, and ambulances. State troopers held back a crowd of curious onlookers, drawn from nearby houses and late-night cafés by the crash.

The darkness was lit by the *whoosh* of

flames as the Cadillac's gas tank exploded.

The crowd that had gathered backed up in horror. "The driver's still in there!" someone yelled.

The crowd pressed forward again as the flames died down. The state troopers pressed them back as two firemen ran toward the Cadillac with a powerful saw and a hydraulic "jaws of life" machine. Two paramedics followed with a gurney.

There was a screech of metal and a crack as the door was popped off the Cadillac. The blackened body that the paramedics pulled out was clearly finished.

No one even bothered to check for a pulse.

The dead man was zipped into a black plastic body bag.

The crowd watched it all with silent curiosity.

Then a middle-aged man in a dark suit and a ten-year-old boy pushed to the front of the crowd.

"It's that tent preacher," someone whispered.

"Excuse me," said the man. "Let us through, please, thank you . . ."

The crowd parted like the Red Sea. This was the Bible Belt, where preachers were respected.

Paramedics wheeled the gurney with the body bag toward a waiting ambulance.

The fire chief flagged them down. "What's going on?" he shouted.

"This one's dead," said a paramedic.

The chief pointed toward the van, crumpled against the curb across the street.

One dazed passenger was throwing up alongside the road. Another was lying on the street, gasping for breath.

"Well, there's a woman over there who isn't dead," the chief told him. "And she needs some oxygen!"

"Yes, sir!"

Leaving the gurney in the middle of the street, the paramedics headed for the van.

"More water! Over there!"

The chief was giving orders to his firemen,

who were dousing the last of the flames inside the Cadillac.

He didn't see the preacher and the boy duck through the police line and approach the gurney.

The preacher unzipped the body bag.

The charred thing inside no longer had a human face. It had been burned beyond recognition. Choking back nausea, the preacher turned away.

The sight didn't seem to bother the boy, though. He reached into the body bag and laid his hands on the brow of the burned head. He then closed his eyes and began to speak in a high, squeaky child's voice. It was somewhere between a prayer and a command.

"I want you to rise!" he proclaimed. "Rise up and be healed!"

A rustle of nervous laughter went through the crowd. They couldn't believe what they were seeing. This weird kid, touching a dead body. Hollering at it . . .

The fire chief looked around and saw the

preacher and the boy. He saw the boy's hands inside the body bag.

"What the hell are you doing?" he demanded.

"The boy is laying on hands," said the preacher. He spoke with a Southern drawl with a backwoods twang.

"Rise up!" the boy cried out, his voice quivering with excitement. "Accept the miracle He has given you, and forsake Him not."

The crowd stopped laughing and grew quiet. A few people pushed forward to see what would happen.

"You don't understand," said the chief. He spoke to the preacher in a calm, deliberate voice, as if he were explaining something to a child. "This man is *dead*."

"Then the boy can't possibly do any harm, can he?" the preacher asked.

Shaking his head with disgust, the fire chief turned away. No point getting into a fight with a preacher, not with a crowd looking on. These people took their religion seriously.

"For this is the power of belief," the boy was saying. "The power to separate the light from the darkness. To create life from death . . ."

The chief had heard enough. He vented his frustration on the crowd. "All right, everybody!" he shouted, waving his arms. "Show's over! Let's clear the area."

The crowd moved back slowly. Reluctantly.

Suddenly, a gasp—and the crowd stopped backing up.

The fire chief looked behind him.

A hand was rising out of the body bag. A crisp, burned, blackened hand.

The hand reached for the boy—and the boy took the gnarled, twisted fingers in his own.

"Hallelujah, Samuel!" cried the preacher. His eyes were shining with tears.

A few amens were murmured in the crowd as people shook their heads in wonder and amazement.

The boy was grinning in triumph.

THE X FILES™

Ruins

A novel by Kevin J. Anderson
Based on the television series created by Chris Carter.

LOST CITY, FOUND
When a well-connected American archaeologist, Cassandra Rubicon, disappears while exploring the lost Mayan city of Xitaclan, the incident becomes a case for FBI agents Mulder and Scully. They are investigators assigned to the X-Files, the strange and inexplicable cases the FBI wants to keep hidden – cases involving the paranormal, the supernatural, and possibly, the extraterrestrial.

Mulder thinks there may be more to this case than simply a missing team of scientists – namely ancient curses, blood sacrifices and deadly reptilian monsters lost in the jungle since before history.

Scully is, as always, more sceptical and likely to provide the logical explanations for her partner's unorthodox speculations. Meanwhile, a covert U.S. military commando team has been sent to investigate, and destroy, a strange electronic signal received from beneath the ruins – a signal aimed upward, at the stars ...

0 00 648253 8

THE X FILES™

Antibodies

A novel by Kevin J. Anderson
Based on the television series created by Chris Carter.

When a disease-ravaged body is found in the smouldering ruins of the DyMar genetic research lab, FBI agents Fox Mulder and Dana Scully fear that a deadly man-made plague is on the loose. As the agents investigating the X-Files – cases that the bureau deem unsolvable – Mulder and Scully must pursue the truth wherever it leads, even into the labyrinthine corridors of the FBI ... and beyond.

Racing to contain the lethal virus before it can spread, Mulder and Scully make a chilling discovery about the lab's most recent project: a promising but highly-dangerous bio-machine that can cure any disease and heal any wound, potentially even a doorway to immortality. But when a second corpse turns up, savagely mutilated from within, it's anything but theoretical. Could machines created to cure have learned to kill? As sinister forces close in, Scully fights to save the life of an innocent boy while Mulder comes face-to-face with a crazed and desperate man whose slightest touch brings agonizing death – and perhaps a resurrection more horrible still.

0 00 648252 X